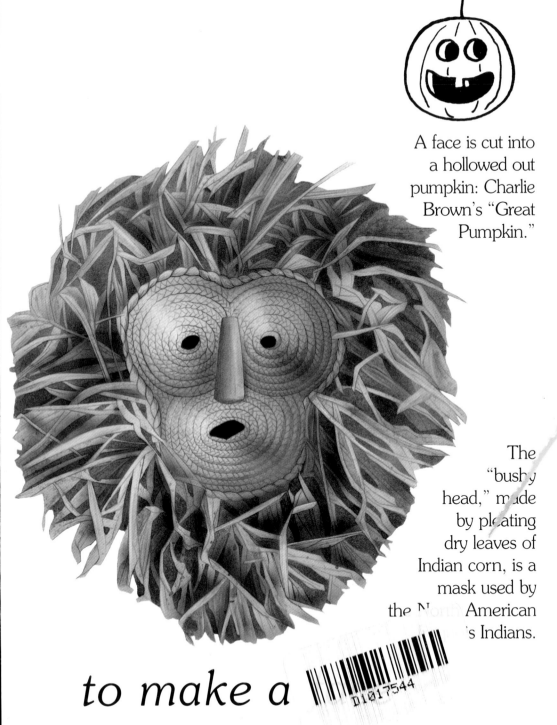

A face is cut into a hollowed out pumpkin: Charlie Brown's "Great Pumpkin."

The "bushy head," made by pleating dry leaves of Indian corn, is a mask used by the North American 's Indians.

to make a

faces can be simple

The face in relief on this small bronze plaque comes from Sicily and is very old; in fact it's 2,700 years old.

This portrait of a woman is by Pablo Picasso, another famous Spanish painter, and was made the same year as the picture by Mirò you saw before.

art for children

the many faces of the face

by
Brigitte Baumbusch

Stewart, Tabori & Chang
NEW YORK

it doesn't take much

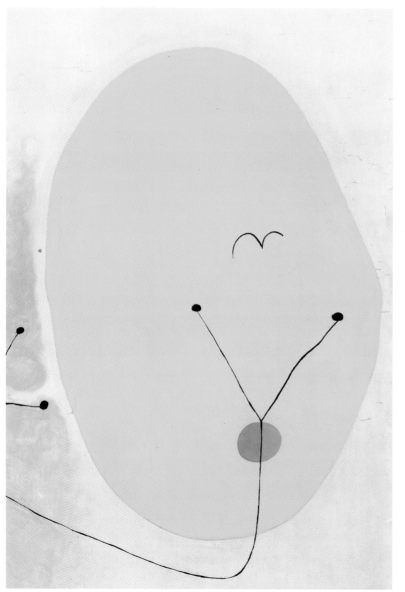

This egg-shaped face was drawn by the Spanish painter Joan Mirò about sixty years ago.

Sometimes an Easter egg has a face too.

or complicated

there are **big** faces

and *small* ones

The enormous head carved from basalt is a sculpture of an Olmec king. Thousands of years ago, the Olmecs lived in Central America, in what is now Mexico.

The little head, made of colored glass, was a charm worn on a necklace. It was made by the Phoenicians, a merchant people, who sailed the Mediterranean Sea in ancient times.

Here is a round vessel made of terra cotta–a kind of water bottle made by many South American peoples.

*some faces are r**O**und*

others

are

long

This portrait of
a woman was painted
by Amedeo Modigliani,
an Italian artist who
lived in Paris at the
beginning of the
twentieth century.

there are famous faces

The *Mona Lisa*
by Leonardo da Vinci
is one of the most famous
paintings in the world and
it's in one of the world's
largest museums: the
Louvre in Paris.

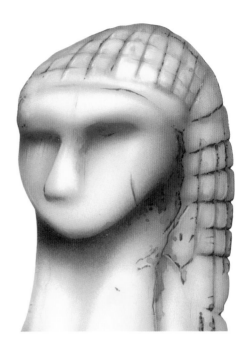

The small head of a
lady dates to the Stone
Age. It was carved
about 20,000 years ago
from a mammoth tusk.

The jar in the form of a man's
head comes from Jericho near
the Dead Sea and was made more
than 3,500 years ago. But Jericho,
which may be the oldest city in the
world, existed way before that.

and nameless ones

faces can be serious

This portrait of Sigmund Freud, the famous Viennese doctor, was painted by modern American artist Ben Shahn. Freud was an expert in interpreting dreams.

or funny

The laughing face on the handle of the stick is a jester. The jester's job was to make people laugh, just like comedians today.

Leonardo da Vinci, one of the greatest artists of the Renaissance, not only painted famous masterpieces like the *Mona Lisa*, but also drew caricatures.

15

... *happy*

This beautiful lady's face was carved in ivory. It was found in the ancient Assyrian town of Nimrud. It may be the portrait of a queen.

About 3,000 years ago, the Assyrian kingdom stretched from the river Tigris to the Mediterranean Sea (modern Iraq and Syria).

This weeping girl is really Saint Mary Magdalen of the Bible who is repenting her sins. Caravaggio, who painted her, was not well regarded in his time because he used ordinary people as models for saints.

or sad ...

sometimes faces are ...

The medieval mind was fond of imagining monsters like this creature. It's a man with his face on his chest.

... out of place

Giuseppe Arcimboldo,
an artist who lived four
centuries ago, amused himself
by painting faces made of
flowers or fruit and vegetables,
animals, books and many
other things. As a joke he
painted this picture of a
vegetable basket which
becomes a face when it's
turned upside down.

faces change with age

At right is *The Three Ages of Man* by Giorgione, a great Venetian painter of the Renaissance. It's a portrait of the same man as a child, a young man and an old man.

... and with

This picture, painted by the Frenchman Louis-Léopold Boilly in the early nineteenth century, gives us a catalog of faces showing various emotions.

feelings !!!

Sally, Charlie Brown's little sister, has an *extremely expressive* face. It's easy to see if she's happy, thoughtful, embarrassed, frightened, angry or furious.

animals have faces too

The picture on the opposite page is titled *I and the Village* and describes life in the Russian countryside. In the foreground are a man and a cow looking at each other. Marc Chagall, who painted it in 1911, was born in Russia, although he then lived in France and in the United States.

This tiger head is Chinese and was made more than 2,000 years ago. It is in bronze with decorations in silver.

even cars may look

This toy made
in the 1950s is a model of a Pontiac,
an American car.

as if they have faces

and the faces of houses

These houses were painted by Henri Rousseau, known as "Le Douanier" (The Customs Officer) because that is what he did for a living. He lived in Paris around a hundred years ago. He was not a professional artist but painted because that was what he liked to do best. Artists like this are called "naive" or "outsider."

are called façades

Picture list

page 4
Joan Miró (1893-1983): *Portrait*, detail,
1938. Zürich, Kunsthaus. Museum photo.
© Joan Miró by SIAE, 1999.

page 5
Pleated mask of the "Corn Face"
or "Bushy Head" society. Iroquois
Indians (Seneca) of the State of New York.
New York, Museum of the American Indian.
Drawing by Lorenzo Cecchi.

The Great Pumpkin from the comic
strip "Peanuts" by Charles M. Schulz
has been reproduced with the kind
permission of Peanuts © United Feature
Syndicate Inc.

page 6
Bronze plaque with a simplified human
face in repoussé. Iron Age, 8th century B.C.,
from Mendalito di Adrano (Sicily).
Syracuse, Archaeological Museum.
Drawing by Luigi Ieracitano.

page 7
Pablo Picasso (1881-1973): *Seated Woman*,
1938. Private property. Photo Scala Archives.
© Pablo Picasso by SIAE, 1999.

page 8
Colossal head in basalt, known as
"The King." Olmec civilization, around
1200 B.C. San Lorenzo, Veracruz (Mexico).
Drawing by Lorenzo Cecchi.

page 9
Small head in colored glass. Carthaginian art,
4th-3rd century B.C. Cagliari, Archaeological
Museum. Drawing by Paola Ravaglia.

page 10
Terra cotta vessel reproducing a human face.
Nazca civilization (Peru), first centuries A.D.
Private property. Drawing by Lorenzo Cecchi.

page 11
Amedeo Modigliani (1884-1920): *Gypsy with a
Baby*, detail, 1919. Washington, National Gallery
of Art, Chester Dale Collection. Museum photo.

page 12
Leonardo da Vinci (1452-1519): *Mona Lisa*.
Paris, Louvre. Photo Scala Archives.

page 13
Small head of a woman in mammoth tusk.
Gravettian, c. 18,000 B.C., from Brassempouy,
Landes (France). Saint-Germain-en-Laye,
Musée des Antiquités Nationales. Drawing
by Lorenzo Cecchi.

Anthropomorphic vase in terra cotta.
Canaanite art, 18th-17th century B.C., from
Jericho. Jerusalem, Israel Museum. Drawing
by Lorenzo Cecchi.

page 14
Ben Shahn (1898-1969): *Portrait of Sigmund
Freud*, 1956. Private property. Photo Scala
Archives. © Ben Shahn by SIAE, 1999.

page 15
Leonardo da Vinci (1452-1519): *Seven Grotesque Heads*, detail. Venice, Academy. Photo Scala Archives.

Jester's stick in wood. French art of the 15th century. Florence, Bargello Museum. Drawing Studio Stalio / Alessandro Cantucci.

page 16
Head of a woman in ivory. Assyrian art, 8th century B.C., from Nimrud. Baghdad, Iraq Museum. Drawing Studio Stalio / Alessandro Cantucci.

page 17
Caravaggio (1571-1610): *The Magdalen*, detail. Rome, Galleria Doria Pamphilj. Photo Scala Archives.

page 18
Nicolò (12th century): relief with an imaginary creature. Detail of the jamb of the portal of the cathedral of Ferrara (Italy). Drawing Studio Stalio / Alessandro Cantucci.

page 19
Giuseppe Arcimboldo (1527-1593): *The Gardener*. Cremona, Museo Civico. Photo Scala Archives.

page 20-21
Giorgione (1477-1510): *The Three Ages of Man*. Florence, Galleria Palatina, Pitti Palace. Photo Scala Archives.

page 22
Louis-Léopold Boilly (1761-1845): *Study of Thirty-Five Facial Expressions*. Tourcoing, Musée des Beaux-Arts. Museum photo.

page 23
The sequence of various frames of Sally from the comic strip "Peanuts" by Charles M. Schulz has been reproduced with the kind permission of Peanuts © United Feature Syndicate Inc.

page 24
Marc Chagall (1887-1985): *I and the Village*, 1911. New York, The Museum of Modern Art. Museum photo. © Marc Chagall by SIAE, 1999.

page 25
Tiger head in bronze with silver inlay. Chinese art, eastern Chou dynasty, 3rd century B.C. Cologne, Museum für Ostasiatische Kunst. Drawing by Lorenzo Cecchi.

page 26
Tin toy of 1954 reproducing a Pontiac Star Chief. Yokohama, Teruhisa Kitahara Tin Toy Museum. Drawing by Lorenzo Cecchi.

page 27
Henri Rousseau (1844-1910): *Landscape with Arch and Three Houses*, detail. Paris, Musée de l'Orangerie. Photo Scala Archives.